Daddy's T-shirt

Lynette Samuel, Author

Leigh Capps, Illustrator

Patty Baker, Creative Consultant

Bright Lamb Publishers

BOOKS TO STRENGTHEN RELATIONSHIPS

To Kyla, Krystal, Jade,
Stuart, Sarah, Samuel,
and Abigail

Daddy's T-shirt
Copyright © 1996 Bright Lamb Publishers

Bright Lamb Publishers, Ltd., P.O. Box 844, Evans, GA 30809.
1 2 3 4 5 6 7 8 9 10
***

First Edition

Library of Congress Cataloging-in-Publication Data:
Library of Congress Catalog Number: 96-83754
Samuel, Lynette
       Daddy's T-shirt / by Lynette Samuel; illustrated by Leigh Capps

Summary: Dad's t-shirts are missing and no one is talking. He begins a search because he is determined to find them.

ISBN 0-9651270-0-1 (book) — ISBN 0-9651270-1-X (package)
[1. T-Shirts — Fiction. 2. Families — Fiction. 3. Dad — Fiction.]
I. Capps, Leigh, ill. II. Title

My Dad is terrific.
Everyone in my house thinks
he's a great guy.

5

Mom loves my Dad.
He helps around the house.
He makes the most delicious
hamburgers on the grill and
the best cheese omelets for
Sunday brunch.

He's there when we need to talk and gives wise advice about problems at school and stuff.

Dad is up bright and early every morning. He takes a nice hot shower and puts on a clean white t-shirt. One day, as Dad was dressing, he noticed that he was running out of t-shirts.

"Honey," he called to Mom, "Where are all of my t-shirts? They seem to be disappearing."

We glanced at each other with guilty grins as Mom quickly replied, "Well, I suppose you'll have to buy some new ones."

You see, we use Daddy's t-shirts for all sorts of things. Come on, I'll show you what I mean.

When my brother needed a smock for art class, Mom
gave him one of Dad's t-shirts. It made a perfect
cover-up. The big shirt protected him
from his neck to his knees. It caught
all the splashes, splatters and spills of
reds, yellows, blues and greens that
sprinkled from his paint brush.

One Saturday afternoon, I watched Mom cut up Dad's old t-shirts to use as dust cloths. With a little rub and a little swish the furniture was sparkling clean.

One very cold and snowy winter morning while Mom was dressing, I noticed that she was putting on one of Dad's t-shirts under her sweater.

"Mommy, why are you wearing Daddy's t-shirt?" I asked.

"Oh, it's so cold outside, Pumpkin. It helps to keep me warm," she answered, tucking the long shirt into her jeans.

I remember the summer reading club at the library where we learned about dinosaurs. The best part was making dinosaurs on our own t-shirts. I used one of Dad's and painted a large brontosaurus on the front.

I love wearing my dinosaur t-shirt to the beach. I think Dad noticed
my t-shirt when we were making sand castles. But I just kept
humming away, enjoying the sun and the sound of the waves.

My big sister wears Daddy's t-shirt to make her outfits look fancy. She buys special paints and glitters to make her own designs. Sometimes flowers, sometimes swirls and twirls. No one ever guesses these were once Dad's plain old t-shirts.

One evening, my sister was on her way to a party. She was wearing one of her specially designed t-shirts. "See you later, Dad," she shouted on her way out.

Dad started to say good-bye. But he stopped, raised his eyebrows and looked twice. Then he just shook his head and mumbled, "Impossible... it couldn't be."

For our spring play last year, my class wore tie-dyed t-shirts for costumes. It was fantastic! When our families came to see the show, none of the Dads knew we were wearing their t-shirts.

Class Play

Now Mom always talks about how important it is to recycle. Dad washes the car with rags from his old t-shirts and he doesn't even know it!

20

You see, Daddy's t-shirts get
cut up,
painted on,
and splattered on.

We rip them,
snip them,
use them,
and abuse them.

I don't know what we would
do without them.

One day, Dad decided that he had run out of
t-shirts for the last time. He started looking
everywhere. I had never seen him so busy.
He spent a whole day
hunting, searching,
sneaking and peeking…

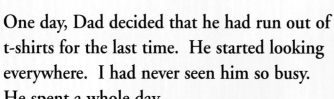

…under the bed, inside
the laundry hamper,
up in the attic, down
in the basement.

We saw Dad crouched
under, bent over,
twisted and coiled in the
most unusual places.

He didn't find his
t-shirts, but he did find
a coat button I'd lost a long
time ago. "Thank you," Mom said
when he found her earring that had
been missing for months.

Dad found everything that had ever been lost
in our house. We were delighted. He was not.

Dad finally gave up and asked for help. "Okay, I need a search party... everybody..." Before he could finish, the excuses came from everyone and everywhere. We suddenly had things to do and places to go.

"Sorry Dad, I'm on my way to the library."

"Soccer practice... gotta go."

"I have too much homework."

"I'm meeting a friend."

Dad was disappointed, but he didn't give up. That evening we thought he had gone too far. Spread before him on the table was: a map of our neighborhood, a blueprint of our house, a magnifying glass, a book on solving mysteries, spectacles on the tip of his nose, and a funny looking hat on his head.

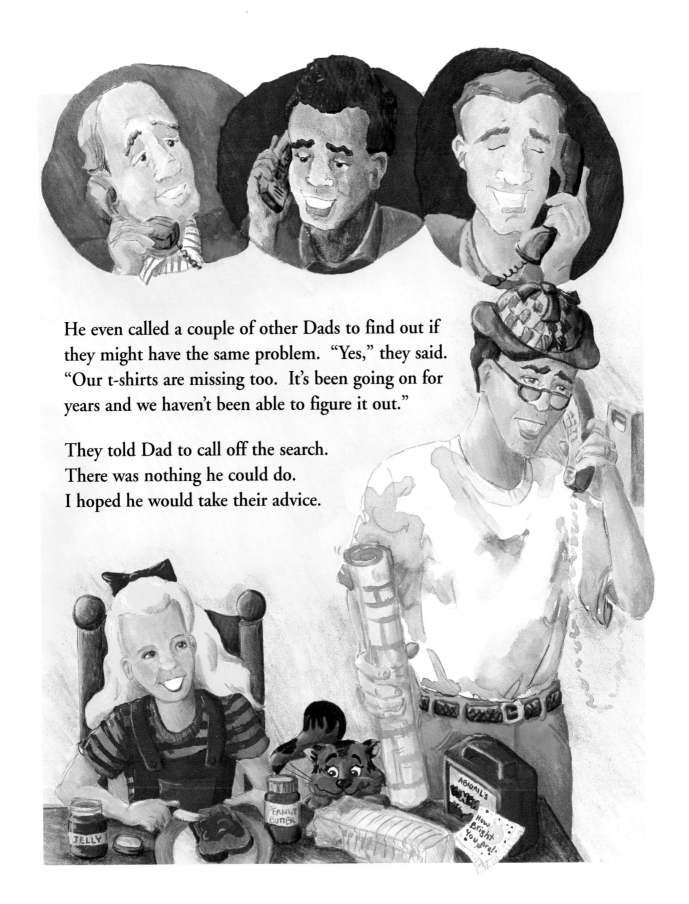

He even called a couple of other Dads to find out if they might have the same problem. "Yes," they said. "Our t-shirts are missing too. It's been going on for years and we haven't been able to figure it out."

They told Dad to call off the search.
There was nothing he could do.
I hoped he would take their advice.

25

One night, when the house was quiet, Dad came to
tuck me into bed.

"How's my favorite little girl?" he asked.

"Fine," I said. "How's my favorite Dad?"

But Dad didn't answer. He squinted his eyes, wrinkled
his forehead, rubbed his chin and scratched his head.

"What's the matter, Dad?"

"Your pajamas… they look a little… um… familiar."

I giggled, slid further underneath my
covers and brought the blanket all the
way up to my chin.

But Dad was quick, he picked me up and out of my bed, swung me high in the air above his head as he exclaimed, "So, you're the one who's been making my t-shirts disappear! I've caught you! I knew there was something funny going on around here!"

He tossed me on the bed and tickled me as I screamed with laughter. Then Dad tucked me in and gave me a big kiss. "I love you, Dad," I said. "I love you too, Pumpkin," he answered.

As I dozed off to sleep, I thought about how special Dad is to us.
I thought about how kind and handsome he is and how important his
family is to him. I thought about all the ways that we use Daddy's
t-shirts. My most favorite is sleeping in them. I feel so warm...
safe... and cozy...

(Totally Awesome Cat ™)